ALSO BY GARY PAULSEN

GARY PAULSEN

OR, The **STRIPPER** and the **STATE**;

How My Mother Started a War with the

SYSTEM That Made Us Kind of

RICH and a Little Bit **FAMOUS**

WENDY
LAMB
BOOKS

Published by
Wendy Lamb Books
an imprint of
Random House Children's Books
a division of Random House, Inc.
New York

Visit us on the Web! www.randomhouse.com/kids
Educators and librarians, for a variety of teaching tools,
visit us at www.randomhouse.com/teachers

Library of Congress Cataloging-in-Publication Data
Paulsen, Gary.
    The glass cafe / Gary Paulsen.
        p. cm.
    Summary: When twelve-year-old Tony, a talented artist,
begins sketching the dancers at the Kitty Kat Club where his
mother is an exotic dancer, it sparks the attention of social
services.
    ISBN 0-385-32499-5—ISBN 0-385-90121-6 (lib. binding)
    [1. Mothers and sons—Fiction. 2. Stripteasers—Fiction.
3. Police—Fiction.] I. Title.
PZ7.P2843Gl 2003
    [Fic]—dc21
2002013582

The text of this book is set in 11-point Leawood.

Book design by Marci Senders

Printed in the United States of America

June 2003

10 9 8 7 6 5 4 3 2

BTP

This book is dedicated to Wanda.

FOREWORD

Which I at first thought was spelled Forward because it was in the beginning or forward part of the book but which the editor corrected. It's the first words, or the forewords. The editor also corrected some other things I did wrong in the story, spelling things that my mother, Al, said were sloppy on my part.

FOREWORD

And tried to make me tone things down because they said it was unbelievable but I wouldn't because the story is all true and happened to me and is mine. And of course Al's. And Miles' and Waylon's and the biker's and don't forget the state's. I mean, like I said in the title.

Thank you,

Your friend,

Tony

CHAPTER ONE

So you know my name is Tony and I am twelve and my mother who is named Alice except nobody calls her that, they all call her Al, like she was a guy only she isn't, is a stripper, only it's called exotic dancing, at a club called the Kitty Kat, except that everybody calls it the Zoo on account of an animal act they used to have but don't anymore because the humane society said it was wrong to use snakes out of their "natural element" although Muriel, who danced with a seven-foot boa named Steve, swore that the snake slept through the whole dance except I know Steve who lives in the dressing room in a glass case and I can't tell if he's sleeping or not because he never closes his eyes.

This is what I like.

I like double bacon cheeseburgers and vanilla shakes.

I like school where I get pretty good grades in everything except gym and sometimes math when it doesn't make any sense to me like when we have to figure out two trains traveling

THE GLASS CAFÉ

at different speeds and which one will get to a place called Parkerville first. There is never a place called Parkerville in real life and hardly any trains go anywhere anymore and why would two trains be trying to get to a place called Parkerville in the first place? It's just silly.

I like Melissa Davidson who is twelve and has short hair and sparks and crackles when she gets mad. A lot. I mean I like her a lot.

I like art and always carry a sketch pad and a couple of soft pencils and draw every chance I get, which is really how the trouble started but I'll talk more about that later after I do what Ms. Providge the English teacher calls "developing the structure and character" of the story. This story. This story about my life.

GARY PAULSEN

I like dogs except that I'm not supposed to have one because the apartment we live in won't allow pets which doesn't seem right because they allow a biker and his woman to live there and a dog is a lot cleaner than a biker. Or at least this biker, who is named Short Man and is so dumb he tried to drink gasoline one day just because it was in a beer bottle and he spit it out on a lit barbecue grill and there were barbecued chicken parts all over the apartment compound and I heard he didn't have a hair left on his head. I know plenty of dogs smarter than that. So I keep trying on the dog thing, doing what Al calls pushing the envelope by bringing them to visit sometimes. Or to be honest every chance I get.

THE GLASS CAFÉ

I like Corvettes. I know it's not cool to like them as much as foreign cars but I read the car magazines in the drugstore owned by Foo Won on the corner when he doesn't catch me. Corvettes, it said in one article I read, are a Greatly Underestimated Force to be Reckoned with in the Muscle Car Arena. Of course I don't have a Corvette but Al said if I want one bad enough and work hard enough I can have one someday when I'm old enough to drive. I would like to have a good car for the muscle car arena.

I like baseball and my favorite team changes some because it started with the Braves and then went to the Padres and then the Yankees and now I'm back to the Braves but I'm definitely leaning back toward the Padres.

I do not like skateboards, or I should say I guess I like them but I don't skateboard anymore because I tried it once without a helmet and hit the concrete so hard I saw flashes of color from one Wednesday to Friday in the next week. I didn't dare to tell Al because she would have taken me to the doctor which she does even if I'm a little sick and not seeing flashes of colors in my head.

I like bicycling. I have an old clunker Schwinn five-speed that looks so bad nobody will steal it except that I took it all apart and the bearings and all the internal parts are slick and new.

I like Coke, not the kind you snort up your nose like Magdalene did until Al got her into treatment and she has two years and two months straight now but the kind you drink from a bottle and I put peanuts in the bottle and drink the Coke and eat the peanuts.

I like Fiji. That's an island country in the South Pacific and I read all about it in a travel magazine at Foo Won's store. I'll go there someday when I am (a) an adult, (b) successful and (c) have a Corvette and maybe (d) married to Melissa which is all part of the list I have for my Life Plan. I don't want to live in Fiji but just visit there after I am certified on scuba gear and can dive, because the diving is supposed to be absolutely stellar there according to the magazine although I always thought stellar meant something to do with the stars.

I do not like television but I used to like TV until Al said it was sucking the brain out of me and hit the set in just the right place to kill it with a small hammer we use to unstick the kitchen window when it's hot and we want it open because the air conditioner only cools the living room and doesn't blow into the kitchen and now it doesn't work. The TV I mean. It hisses and pops but there's no picture or sound. Then Al made me go with her to the library and I got dozens of books even though I didn't read much then but do now and twice a week we have literary discussion evenings about books we have both read that week. We never had television discussion evenings twice a week when I watched TV and now I don't like it anymore. TV I mean. And I don't watch it at all even when I'm visiting Waylon who is my best outside friend and who is twelve and who has television and is maybe even a tube head and also does not have television or literary discussion evenings twice a week in his home. I think mostly because Waylon says his folks both work hard and are never really home. But Al works hard too, and is home almost all the time when she isn't working.

I like Waylon outside. Inside he mostly just sits around and talks about what he wants to do outside but outside he's great on a bike when we want to ride the four miles down to the beach and watch the ocean or the beach freaks or the jugglers or the beach dogs working their

Frisbees or taking balls out of the surf and we eat those rubbery hot dogs in limp buns which only taste good at the beach and I can never tell Al I ate because she says they're made out of sheep's eyeballs and testicles and petroleum byproducts and will make my liver rot before I'm sixteen which she says is a very bad age to have a rotten liver. Waylon is the best friend for all that and one inside thing too, the computer. Waylon is very good with a computer and sometimes we'll sit in my house and work the Net. Al, who says the computer is good but not all parts of the Net are good, limits me to one hour a day on the Net and if I do more or if she catches me looking for porno sites she says she will take the little hammer we use on the kitchen window and tap the computer in just the right place to kill it. She likes that hammer and talked once about using it on the biker when he said something snotty I didn't catch as we walked by but he must have believed her because he's been nice ever since.

And I like Al. I mean I know you're supposed to like your mother or love your mother but I mean I like Al who never wants me to call her Mother or Mom or Ma but just Al like a friend, a best friend, better than Waylon even outside and Al is good both outside and inside and sometimes when it's the worst day of my whole life and maybe Melissa is talking about somebody else or math is kicking my butt or I have a cold and the smog is making it worse

Al can just laugh, a deep laugh that comes from way inside and I can't help but smile and think of something good. Which makes what happened because of the drawings really, really stupid.

CHAPTER TWO

The thing is right about here if we followed Ms. Providge's rules for English we would probably move on to the plot, where the characters have what she calls "conflict," and we would work through the "conflict" to some "form of resolution."

And I would like to do that, I really would

except that I think it would leave out the most important thing which is that if we jump right to the conflict part where we try for a resolution you would miss most of my life which is really maybe the most important part because that's the part the state just couldn't understand and was why Al got mad and made them mad and that brought in the cops which freaked out the biker who became a one-man "armed camp" according to the *Los Angeles Times* which made a SWAT team Respond and React which destroyed a perfectly good door belonging to Juan Gomez who was only a little bit illegal involving the immigration aspect of life.

But all that's for later when we get to the part about conflict and plot resolution.

THE GLASS CAFÉ

For now I think I should maybe talk about my day. On school days I get up at seven o'clock and Al gets up and we have pancakes. Every school morning. Al is there every morning when I go to school and every afternoon when I come home. Sometimes in the mornings she's a little slow waking up because she works so late. We make pancakes from a mix and I have three cakes and she has one because, as she says, her figure is important to our livelihood, with light maple syrup except they call it "Lite Surrupp" on the bottle which is just wrong, just plain wrong even if they're trying to be cute. Then I sip a juice while she drinks a cup of coffee, black of course because of calories which she thinks of as a kind of bug that can kill you, as if calories were hiding there in food to get you and not just a measurement of heat. We talk about school and how I can improve my math grades and she gives me money for the day, bus money and lunch money, and I take the bus to school. I have small jobs I do for money but she won't let me spend that on lunch or the bus to school because she says that's her responsibility. It seems like a fuzzy line to me and I think I should pay my way and she says I do just by being a kid and shouldn't have to worry about other things and I say that's all right but I'm growing fast and going to be a man someday and should be learning about responsibility myself. She says don't hurry it up it will come soon enough and do I want her to be a grandmother already? I stop arguing then. But I still think I'm right.

I read somewhere that the city doesn't have a good bus system which is why everybody drives all the time which causes all the traffic jams. But the buses are almost always on time and except for a druggie or a jerk now and then there isn't any trouble riding them.

School is like, you know, well, everybody has school so it isn't necessary to get into it too much except to say that there are jocks and jerks and dweebs and geeks and cool people and not cool people and some good teachers and some not so good and the principal is a retired army colonel named Armstrong who at first thought he was still in the army and wanted people to call him Colonel Armstrong, but mellowed out when one morning all the kids stood in formation in the halls and slow-marched one . . . step . . . at . . . a . . . time all in perfect formation from first- to second-period class.

I guess we're about like all middle schools except we have a drama teacher named Miles who gets so intense sometimes he practically faints when he reads Shakespeare and we have to dab his face with damp paper towels and pretend to help him to his desk so he can re-cover. Miles works really hard and does a lot of small parts on television. Waylon says he sees him all the time in commercials and used car ads and he doesn't need to teach, but he really likes kids. He comes once a week to teach drama in case anybody wants to be an actor and says he faints because Shakespeare is so good he takes his, Miles', breath away. I don't have that trouble with Shakespeare yet but I try to read him a little every week because I figure if he can make Miles who is a professional actor faint there must be something to his work.

School sometimes goes very fast like when art is fun or we get to read in English or when history is about war and sometimes, like when there is a math test, it can take forever. But usually the five days of school seems like maybe only seven or eight days and then a weekend comes.

During the week I have to study and do

homework and every night before she goes to work Al sits with me and we go over what I'm supposed to do that night or from the night before if I didn't get it done. She goes to work about seven so she can get ready for the first show which is at eight and she gets home between midnight and one in the morning. I've never been in the club part where she works but have been in the dressing room area and I know most of the girls who work there. I like them and they seem to like me, and I know all their names and most of their measurements because they're on the posters. . . . But more on that later when we talk about how the difficulties started.

On the weekends I have work to do around

the apartment complex for Mr. Haver who is the manager and part owner. I get some money for cleaning the sidewalks and raking the little bit of grass at the front and picking up the trash and then there are chores to do at home, like help clean the house and take out the garbage and of course homework. But some of that can be done during the week. So sometimes Al and I will take the Bug which we restored together using magazines from Foo Won's except for the parts that were too tricky for us, even with the magazines to help us, when we had to go to a machine shop for help, and we head off to sit on the beach so Al can read Charles Dickens who she loves or go up along the highway and have a picnic. But sometimes Al has other stuff to do or a date or has to work both Friday and Saturday night and has to rest a bit Sunday so I'll take off with Waylon on our bikes and we go to the movies or out to the mall where I once saw Mel Gibson get out of a plain old Chevy, not even a limo, or maybe it was somebody who looks just like him, and we'll play some video games or look at stuff we can't afford to buy.

Sometimes when I feel brave I'll call Melissa and ask her if she'd like to go to a movie and about one out of four times she'll say yes which is almost worse than when she says no because then I get scared about what to wear and what to say and how to look and comb or not comb my hair or use cologne or not use cologne or aftershave or not aftershave even though I don't shave. I mean I turn into a mess. I dug into the relationship magazines at Foo Won's and decided that while we're friendly we are nowhere near showing PDA (Public Displays of Affection) and we're a very long way from being MIF (Monogamous in Friendship) and may never get to IWA (Intimate When Alone) and we'll definitely have to pick up the pace a great deal before we enter steps A, B, C and D from my plan, which I haven't told Melissa about yet. According to the articles if I did I might drive her away because she might be CS (Commitment Shy) and not even know it. Many are. That's how they say it in the articles. Many are.

Which is an "aside," as Ms. Providge would put it, and not "germane to the plot" except that it shows me and my "character arc" which I guess is important because it's a story about me. Ms. Providge did not use the words "character arc." That came from Miles when he was describing a role he had in a commercial where he was a man holding a watermelon in back of a customer at a supermarket checkout stand who was taking *forever* to make out a check instead of using a special shopping card and caused Miles to drop the watermelon which splattered all over the floor and Miles said he had only that to use to develop the "character arc" of the man he was supposed to be portraying, just the moment when the watermelon splattered and Miles said it wasn't dramatic enough to have the impact needed for the impatience and anger involved so I guess, thinking about it, that I will never be an actor because I just don't think in dramatic arcs. Which is another aside but we'll leave it in because it's about Miles and I like Miles and he should be in all of this even though he doesn't become a real point of my character arc until the end when he meets Al and there is this spark thing that happens between Miles and Al that I would like to have happen with Melissa and me only it hasn't. Yet.

We go to movies a lot, Waylon and I, although I'm trying to expand my mind because of Melissa, and Waylon only wants movies where things blow up or get shot. I don't mind that and once in math class as a kind of exercise I thought of all the movies I went to and made a table and found that as a general thing I need three or four movies about things blowing up or somebody getting shot for every movie that I might be able to take Melissa to see which would be a movie about a girl who was never popular in school suddenly finding a way to get popular and be dated by the captain of the football team or her father buys her a Camaro or a Porsche and she saves a dolphin or maybe all of the above, which I think would be an ideal movie for someone like Melissa. I don't mean to sound bitter but sometimes I have a tough time staying awake when I go to a Melissa-type movie and it would be so much easier if a lot of things happened much faster. Like maybe the Camaro, which a lot of people think is hot but which in my opinion is not a particularly good car for the muscle car arena, could blow up. Or maybe the captain of the football team could go insane and shoot at a dolphin or a whale and the boy who wasn't all that popular but who knew a lot about cars because he read all the car magazines at Foo Won's could drive like a true professional muscle car driver and save the dolphin or the whale and the girl would be so grateful she would see the error of her ways and like the guy who wasn't all that popular but was better than the football player who shot dolphins or whales.

That's what Ms. Providge would call a fantasy and not at all germane to the plot but I think Miles would say it applied to my character arc so I'll leave it in.

During the work week the day usually ends with me going to bed and I'm supposed to sleep because Al doesn't get home until late and Mr. and Mrs. Gomez check on me to make sure everything is all right which is all just for Al because I can and do take care of myself but I never go to sleep, not once, until Al comes home although I pretend to be asleep when she comes to my room and checks me and kisses me on the forehead and tucks the covers in because I don't want her to worry and that is the way my day ends.

Except of course until everything went to pieces.

CHAPTER THREE

I'm not going to blame art because art isn't a thing that can be blamed but that's what started it. Art, pure and simple, because I love drawing and I was sitting in art class one day and Ms. Klein who teaches art was talking about figure studies. Ms. Klein has a way of getting excited about what she teaches so that everybody or nearly everybody in her class gets excited along with her and she had brought in a book from home that was about figure drawing and she passed the book around to the class and she said:

"All great artists spend much of their time studying and painting the human figure."

The book was all figures, mostly nude except not in what Ms. Providge would call a "provocative" way except of course some of the boys who weren't into art giggled and pointed at bare parts but when the book came to me a strange thing happened.

I decided to be an artist.

I don't mean I thought I was great or would ever be great or would grow up to do A, B, C and D as an artist. I mean I decided that I would always like art and would always do art even if I did something else for a living like be a muscle car racer or a doctor or a rich person, which has always intrigued me—just being a rich person, but that's an aside—and so I decided I had to begin to study the human figure.

Ms. Klein talked all that day about figure drawing and when the book had gone around I went up front and studied it and I found that most of the artists must have decided the female figure was better for drawing than the male because the drawings of nude women outnumbered the drawings of nude men about eleven to one. I asked her about it.

"Yes, that's true, and it's strange. It was

much easier to get men to model than women. Michelangelo had to use male bodies for models for female sculpture because he could not get any women to pose nude, which made for some strange-looking women, and yet even with that most artists preferred painting the feminine figure. Perhaps because they have better lines, more active and curving lines. In my life drawing classes, we use mostly women."

Well, I thought, I won't have a problem there because of all the girls I knew who worked with Al. Of course they weren't girls at all but Al always called them that. That night I asked Al at dinner if I could come to the club some night and do some sketches of the girls.

THE GLASS CAFÉ

She studied me for a long time. "You can't come in the club proper—you're too young."

"Just in the dressing room. And only if they don't mind."

Another look, a long look. "And this is really just for art class?"

I shook my head. "Not only. I saw the book and this feeling came over me like no matter what I did with my life I should be an artist and Ms. Klein said that all artists study the fig-ure and that you're never too young to start and I thought how great it would be to come to the club and do sketches that I could finish later."

Al asked everyone first if it would be all right and explained that I wouldn't do anything wrong or vulgar. They all agreed that it would be all right and so I took a drawing tablet the next night and sat back in the corner of the dressing room and I want to say right here and now that it's not what some of you are probably thinking.

I mean I am, well, I guess, normal. I mean certain things make me think certain thoughts and cause certain things to happen to certain parts of my body just like anybody else but this was all different.

I mean I knew all these ladies because I've been there before and seen them sometimes with their clothes off or partly off and it wasn't like when those other things happen because of the magazines in Foo Won's or the scenes of some of the shows on television that Waylon watches and I sometimes see.

This was like work or something, like I was suddenly a doctor or, well, maybe an artist because I didn't see the girls as men would see them in the club but somehow I saw inside of what they were:

Muriel leaning on the dressing table dabbing at bits of sweat that were running down her chest between her breasts, her eyes all tired and her makeup messed but a soft smile there too, a smile of knowing something that maybe was a secret or some new thing she had learned, just a soft smile and the curve of her arm as she dabbed with the tissue, that curve and the line of her back and neck and I tried to draw that line, that curve and the look on her face, and it didn't work. Not at first. So I tried again and again and finally I could see the curve working, the line, and that night at home after dinner and homework I took out the sketch tablet and worked on different versions until I thought I had it close and I showed it to Al and she took a sharp breath and looked away and said, "How did you know that?"

"What?"

"That Muriel has hard miles on her. Don't show her the drawing, all right?"

"I didn't know that about her." And I was telling the truth. I didn't know those things but I could see it in the sketch even if it wasn't in my mind so I knew it without knowing it and I went back to the club the next day and didn't take the sketch but did other drawings of Helen by the air cooler blowing into the dressing room with the wind from the cooler moving her hair around her face so the lines didn't show and Patty looking out the back window of the dressing room which was painted black but looking as if she could see things outside anyway and Penny leaning back against the wall by her seat at the dressing table sound asleep, as sound asleep as if she were home in bed and not on a ten-minute break between dances and Sally who was really named Eugenia but took Sally for a stage name sitting nude with a guitar in her lap playing flamenco with her long fingers flying on the strings to

make the chords. I took all the sketches home
and worked on them each night after home
work until I had nine drawings that I though
were as good as I could do. At least as good a
I could do then. I put them in a folder and
took them to class on a Monday and turned
them in to Ms. Klein.

She was busy and so I put the folder on he
desk and I went on to another class without he
having a chance to look at them. I was home
that night sitting at the table with Al talking
about Dickens which wasn't really fair because
she knew everything about him including an
operation he had on his butt before he took a
sea voyage to the United States and how it
made him feel about life and literature and

had only read *A Christmas Carol* once for class. The phone rang and it was Ms. Klein.

"Tony." She said it flat. Like did I know I was Tony.

"Yes." I didn't recognize her voice at first. "This is Tony. Who are you?"

"Oh . . . this is Ms. Klein from art class. I was just looking at your drawings tonight. I brought them home and I was just looking at them, you know, kind of studying them . . ."

She kept sort of repeating herself that way which I'd never heard her do before, and finally she came out with it.

"Did you copy them from someplace?"

I shook my head and then remembered I was on the phone. "No."

"Perhaps from a magazine or an art book?"

"No. I . . . I took them from life." The truth was that nobody at school really knew where Al worked. I wasn't ashamed of it or anything but like Al said, what we did, how we lived was pretty much our own business. I once asked her about my father, why we never heard from him, and she just said, "It's none of his business to know us. He's gone."

"Just exactly what kind of life would that be?" Ms. Klein asked.

"Could you wait a minute?" I held my hand over the phone and turned to Al who was sitting at the kitchen table with a notebook where she'd been writing some different points she wanted to make about Dickens and how he was the first true novelist even though Cervantes and Balzac had done novels before him and Sir Walter Scott but they hadn't really done novels. She said.

"Al," I said, "it's about the pictures I did for art class."

"What about them?"

"Ms. Klein wants to know where I did them."

And here Al made one of those mistakes you make because you don't think there can be anything wrong with the idea. "So tell her."

And I did. There was a long silence on the phone and then Ms. Klein said:

"Your mother works at the Kitty Kat Club?"

"Yes."

"As a waitress?"

"No. She dances there."

"Oh. Is she one of the women in the drawings?"

"No. Those are the other dancers who work there. Why, is there a problem or something?"

"No, no. Tony." Again, like she was telling me my name. "Do you know . . . I mean to say these drawings are really good."

"Well, thank you." Maybe that meant I would get a good grade. That would bring the average up because the math grade would take it down and then I thought, hey, I was using math, figuring the average out and maybe if I thought of it that way, as math being something I could use . . .

"I mean I think these drawings are *very*

good, Tony. I think you really have talent. Is your mother there?"

"Yes."

"Could I speak to her?"

I handed the phone to Al and she said, "Yes?"

And then. "Oh, really?"

And then. "Well, I'm very impressed. Thank you for telling me."

And then. "Well, yes, I'm all right with it but you should talk to Tony."

She handed the phone back to me and Ms. Klein said, "Tony. I want to submit your drawings to a kind of competition at the art museum downtown."

"You mean a contest?" I had never had any

45

luck at contests except one where I drew the head of a pirate that was on the back of an old matchbook and sent it in and a company wanted me to send them money to make me into a top commercial artist but I thought it was strange. If I *won* the contest they shouldn't be asking me for money. So I blew it off. I don't normally say that but it's slang and Ms. Providge says it's all right to use slang now and then because it helps develop the character. My character. Besides, I think it's kind of cool to say it—I just blew it off.

"It's not a contest, really . . . well, perhaps it is at that. You don't compete with others so much as just yourself. If the panel thinks your work is good enough you can get professional training and scholarships."

THE GLASS CAFÉ

"I'll have to ask Al . . . my mom."

"She already said it was all right."

"Oh. Well, if it's okay with her it's okay with me."

Which is just exactly how it started.

CHAPTER FOUR

I don't want to give the impression that everything in my life just stopped when I did the drawings or that we just sat and waited to see what would happen. My life had a character arc before I did the drawings and it kept on arcing and is still arcing.

I found out for instance that maybe Melissa

really liked me but was playing hard to get because she had read in a magazine that boys didn't like girls that came after them and I learned this because she told a girl named Kimberley and Kimberley told a girl named Janice and Janice knew Waylon's sister because Waylon's sister sometimes did baby-sitting for the people next door to Janice and they would sit and talk and talk and talk and Waylon's sister let it slip right after breakfast that she heard from Janice who heard from Kimberley that Melissa liked me and Waylon told me.

You couldn't have known by how she acted. She still would only go to the movies one out of four and sometimes five times I asked but it made me feel good anyway.

THE GLASS CAFÉ

It was along about then when I almost got rich. This is how it happened. I sent in my name on a big publisher form that came in the mail and they sent me back another form. It had a picture of some old guy who used to be on television all the time, saying I was one of sixty people being considered for winning a huge amount of money, over a million dollars, and that if I sent in the next form I would be in the running and I did and they sent me back *another* form saying I was one of only twelve people and they had all the other names there so I thought how it would be great to get in touch with all of them and agree to split the money among the twelve so we'd each get over a hundred thousand dollars. But I couldn't find their addresses so it all kind of fell apart and I didn't win the money. I guess one of the twelve got lucky. There's all that math again. Just about when I think I don't need it some number thing pops up like trying to figure odds or averages or dividing over a million dollars, and I find a use for it. I guess I'll have to work at it harder because I'd hate to be that close on a contest again and not get it right. People will take advantage of you if they think you don't know something. Al says that all the time and she told me she ought to know although she never explains just *why* she ought to know.

But I was close, and that should count for something when it comes to story line and character arc. You can see how I would have acted if I had won the money and that I have certain "character traits," like I'm not really greedy and was perfectly willing to share the money with the other winners and not just run out and buy a Corvette right away. I might even be a little responsible, although I think it's too soon to know that yet.

I got a dog during that time before the world blew up. That's how Al puts it. The world blew up. . . .

I was walking down the street kind of minding my own business having just come from nearly breaking every bone in my body with a pair of Rollerblades Waylon borrowed for the day from his older brother. They were a little too big which might explain why I kept catching the toes and splattering my face all over the sidewalk and I was glad when Waylon took them back to his brother because it was becoming one of those fun things to do that if it got to be just a little more fun it would kill me so I was walking home wondering what to tell Al about all the marks on my face when this brown dog came out of a bush and stuck his nose in the back of my knee. He took a long snuffling breath and wagged his tail and followed me home.

I forgot to say my favorite color is brown back when I was talking about what I like but it is and it was the shade of brown this dog was colored.

He didn't have a collar and kept smelling the

back of my knee and following me so I named him Carlyle because Brownie would be too lame and I had read the name Carlyle in a story and Carlyle followed me home and into the apartment without my really trying.

"What happened to your face and where did you get the dog?" Al was sitting in the kitchen in her terry-cloth bathrobe getting ready to dress for work.

"Rollerblading and he followed me home."

"We can't have pets. You know the rules."

"I named him Carlyle."

"Ummmm."

"I'll take good care of him."

"It's against the rules."

"Well."

She was quiet for a long time. "You think you can hide him from the super?"

I nodded.

"How many will this make?"

I shrugged. "I don't know. Maybe ten, twelve."

"And you get caught every time."

"But I'm getting better at it. Last time it was over a month."

She looked at the dog. "Why is he smelling the back of your knee?"

"I think I fell in something that smells good."

"With the *back* of your knee?"

"I'm not very good with Rollerblades."

"Heaven help us when you get a Corvette."

"That's different. I'll be older."

"Ummmm." And I thought she might be going to say something she says all the time about men just being bigger boys with larger toys but the phone rang. Al never answers the phone if she's busy with something else. It can ring for an hour and she won't pick it up. "It's an invitation, not a command," she says, "and I don't have to answer an invitation."

So I answered it, thinking it might be Waylon or even Melissa though I can't remember a time when she actually just up and called me and this woman's voice said, like she knew I wasn't a man, "Is your mother there?"

"It depends," I said, "on if it's an invitation or a command."

"I beg your pardon?"

"Al doesn't answer commands and usually doesn't want to be invited to talk so when you say 'Is your mother there?' it's kind of a complicated question. If we work it out, and I'm not saying we will work it out, but if we do and we decide she is here do you want to talk to her?"

There wasn't any sound for a long time but I could hear her breathing, like she was thinking about it, and then she took a deep breath and said evenly, "Yes. If we decide she's there I would like to speak with your mother."

"And whom," and I said *whom* and not *who* even though I'm not sure which is right, "should I say is calling?"

"My name is Judith Preston, Mrs. Judith Preston."

THE GLASS CAFÉ

"And the nature of your call?"

Another very long pause. "I'm with the state government and there is a complaint lodged against your mother that we are investigating."

"A complaint?"

"Really, I think it would be more appropriate for me to speak with your mother. She *is* named Alice Henson, is she not?"

She had the name right. Still, Al was getting into her working mood and she didn't like to be interrupted when she was getting ready for work. She said exotic dancing, if it was done right, was a Zen kind of thing and she worked at the music, becoming tuned with the music, before she left home, breathing deeply with her eyes closed and her fingers pressed together before she even went to the club. She told me once that the audience didn't matter unless they touched you and she never allowed anybody to get that close. Conan didn't let them either. He was the bouncer and his mother took his name from a comic book.

Still, it was the state calling. "Hold the line," I said. "I'll see if she's here."

Of course, Al was three feet away. I held my hand over the phone. "It's the state. They say there's a complaint against you but the woman won't tell me what it is or anything about it."

At first I thought she didn't hear me but then she breathed out, opened her eyes and put her hand out for the phone.

"This is Alice Henson."

A pause, then:

THE GLASS CAFÉ

"What is the nature of the complaint?"

Another pause, then:

"That's patently absurd." She smiled and I knew that was because she likes to say that phrase: *patently absurd.*

Another wait, then:

"It is *art,* Mrs. Preston, but if you have to do it tomorrow, eleven in the morning would be best. I work late at night."

Then she handed me the phone to hang up. I did. Then I waited and when it seemed she was never going to say anything I said, "Well?"

"Those sketches you did of the girls were put in a display at the art museum along with a short sentence about you being a young person and some anonymous person saw it and made a complaint to the social services that some-body, meaning me, was allowing their child, meaning you, to draw pornographic pictures."

"You mean they think the sketches of the girls are dirty?"

She nodded. "You heard me—I told her it was art, but she said even so it has to be investigated so she is going to come out tomorrow for what she called a 'preliminary conversation.' "

"That's crazy."

"Patently"—she nodded—"absurd."

CHAPTER FIVE

So what the woman didn't tell us was that she was with the juvenile welfare division of the state and was a caseworker for abused kids. It was her first mistake but it still might not have been so bad if she hadn't done almost everything else she did as wrong as she could do it.

First she did not come alone but arrived accompanied by a policeman. He was nice enough but he was armed and stood too close to me. I could see that it bothered Al right away.

They came exactly at eleven. Al had put on a pair of jeans and a T-shirt and had had her coffee so she was awake and alert and did not like Mrs. Preston from the moment she walked in the door. With an armed man, as Al said later, who never had his hand that far from the butt of his nine-millimeter. Al does not like guns or what guns do or the people who use guns or the people who sell guns or the people who make guns, even guns for hunting, which she thinks is immoral and wrong although I've never heard her call it patently absurd.

"Let's see," Mrs. Preston said, taking out a

folder and a ballpoint pen before she had been there ten seconds. "Your name is Alice Henson?" The pen hung over the paper.

"What is that?" Al asked, her voice cold.

"This," Mrs. Preston said, "is the initial investigation form we must fill out."

"Why must 'we' fill it out?"

Mrs. Preston looked at the policeman and raised her eyebrow as if to say, Oh yeah, one of these smart ones.

"Mrs. Henson, there has been a complaint lodged."

"A complaint about what?"

Another raised eyebrow and I thought, Oh, this is just great—the cop will have to pull them apart in about a minute.

"I think it would be best if Officer Bates took

Anthony into the other room so we can discuss this alone."

"No." Al's voice was cold, seemed to make the room cold. "Officer Bates isn't taking my son anywhere."

Mrs. Preston took a long breath and looked at Officer Bates again, the eyebrow raised again, the almost sneer again. "Look, you don't seem to understand. We're here because a complaint has been filed that you are mistreating your child—"

"No. I'm not."

"—and if we want to or feel it is necessary we can take the child into protective custody."

Al turned an ugly shade of white, almost gray, really, and her eyes got very bright and sparkly, like the time just after the biker said the thing to her that I didn't hear when Al told him about the hammer and then the biker got real nice to us both. I'd only seen her eyes look like that the one time before and, even though things worked out with the biker, this time everything went downhill so fast it seemed like we were riding on a greased sled.

Looking back, I try to make it slow motion in my mind which Miles says he does sometimes when he is rehearsing a scene or a part for a commercial.

First I stepped away from the cop. I think he thought I was going to run when really all I was going to do was get a better view of the fight I was sure was going to start in about half a second between Mrs. Preston and Al. It turned out I had the time right but the target wrong.

As I moved, the policeman reached out for my arm and missed and his hand bounced off my shoulder and hit the side of my head. It wasn't much of a hit—there was no pain or anything—but I must have winced because I saw Al's eyes go bad again and she said a word to the cop which I had heard the biker use on more than one occasion and she swung around and picked up a table lamp and hit the cop across the top of his head so hard it sounded like somebody dropping a watermelon the way Miles did in the commercial.

It's funny but I always thought a lamp would break if you hit somebody over the head with it

THE GLASS CAFÉ

I had seen people getting hit with things like the lamp in movies and the lamp always broke only this time it just went "thunk" and the cop went down on his knees and then down on his face making a sound like the little pump motor in the fish tank in the biology lab at school, which is called a simile, and Mrs. Preston grabbed me and fumbled for a little radio in her purse and yelled the address and then screamed:

"Send backup! She's evading! She's evading!" But I really think what she meant was that Al was resisting because in no way did Al try to evade anything or anybody but instead when she saw that Mrs. Preston was trying to pull me out of the room, she dropped the lamp and came toward us like a tiger except she didn't growl but said another word that I'd heard the biker use. Mrs. Preston was digging in her purse again and brought out a Mace sprayer.

For a second there was some struggling and some more bad language, surprisingly enough from Mrs. Preston this time and then Mrs. Preston leaped back and said, "I've got you now!" and cut loose with the Mace except that it had gotten turned around and she sprayed herself in the face.

Mace smells pretty bad if you're just in the room with it and what with Mrs. Preston taking a full dose in the face and now rolling around on the floor I thought it might be a good time to take Al by the arm and lead her outside for a breath of fresh air.

THE GLASS CAFÉ

Just for the record we did not evade arrest as the paper said later. When backup came it was a SWAT team and we were sitting on the front steps of the apartment and moved over nice as could be so the SWAT team could get by and I think it would all have settled down then except the biker came out of his apartment just as he saw the SWAT team come into the courtyard and he yelled something about black helicopters and ran back into his apartment and came out with a very realistic-looking but plastic toy M-16 which he aimed at the SWAT team and pulled the trigger so the toy made a popping sound and sprayed a plume of water.

I've done some research since and those SWAT men are trained in RR (Rapid Response) and TR (Target Recognition). I think there were just six or seven SWAT team members but it seemed like a couple of hundred and what's amazing is that in all the confusion only one of the policemen didn't instantly realize it was a squirt gun and, in his defense, he only shot Mr. Gomez's door which was next to the biker but did you know—this is an aside—that they don't have to buy you a new door when they shoot one off your house?

Even though the biker was fine and, to be fair, he started it, he started screaming about police brutality and how when he was a baby somebody put a chip in his butt so he could be tracked by satellite wherever he went because they always wanted to know where he was except he never said who "they" was except that they all seem to have black helicopters.

THE GLASS CAFÉ

We were sitting there by the side of the entry when they led him out, chained with his hands to his waist and down to his legs, and I was sort of thinking it was all over when Mrs. Preston came stumbling out of our apartment, rubbed the last of the Mace from her eyes, pointed at Al and me and yelled:

"There they are! It's those two. Assault and resisting arrest. Get them!"

Which is how I came to be arrested and ride in the back of a patrol car with handcuffs and spend the night in a green room with boogers on the wall and a ten-year-old boy named Benny who said he was trying for the world record in stolen bicycles and was over two hundred and fourteen and had only been caught sixty-four times.

CHAPTER SIX

All right so now there has been some character development and a lot of conflict if you consider the cop hitting me and Mrs. Preston pulling me and freaking out Al and the SWAT team shooting Mr. Gomez's door next to the biker but none of that explains how I might come to be the youngest person in

America to own a Corvette if I can talk Al into it, which is giving something away but is done in the interest, as Ms. Providge would say, of "further plot development."

Of course a lot of it has been in the papers and on television which is how I found out I am photogenic although it doesn't matter because I'm never going to be an actor or work in films. But I found out one thing about television and the news media which is that when they write about me or Al and what happened a lot of what they say is just flat wrong, like when they say we were rich, which we weren't then but kind of are now, or when they say everything turned out all right because Al was a close friend of a senator who offered to help us.

THE GLASS CAFÉ

Except that the senator was a woman who Al met in a yoga class and not a man who offered to help us because Al is beautiful and an exotic dancer, like the press said, so it makes you wonder about everything they say, the press I mean.

The truth is we got arrested and held that night and Al called a friend who was a lawyer and the lawyer came down that night and talked the way lawyers talk and in the morning we were released without bail which made me feel all right because I was sick of looking at the boogers on the wall but not all right because I was still talking to Benny about breaking records. Not by stealing bikes, because that was Benny's idea, but I thought breaking a record of some kind might be the way to get famous and rich.

We went home and for a week nothing happened except that the biker stopped me outside one day and held his hand up to slap mine and said:

"Hey, cool, man . . ."

Which I think meant he liked me because I'd been arrested and maybe had a chip in my butt now so I would be tracked by the black helicopters too. But it didn't matter and Waylon and I went down to the beach and spent a day and I went back to school and I thought that was the end of it.

Then Mrs. Preston filed formal charges of assault and resisting arrest against Al and then

added charges of child endangerment and mis-
treatment against Al and the television crews
came to talk to us and the newspapers came
and they spent more time than they would have
spent because I'm a little photogenic but Al,
she's *really* photogenic and knows how to
stand and smile so they kept coming back and
the headlines read:

STRIPPER MOM FIGHTS SYSTEM

And:

MOM BARES ALL FOR ART

And they had some pictures from the
brochures and posters from the club and that
brought the press back again and then they

published the drawings I'd done of the girls and that brought them back again and by the time we were scheduled to go to court for the first hearing everything was completely out of control and the press was there from all over. We had to fight our way into the courthouse and the camera flashes were going off so thick inside I was half blind.

We had spoken to our attorney, a blond man named Wilton, and he was joined by an attorney from the art people who showed my drawings and they were joined by an attorney from an artists' rights group who said our freedom was being infringed upon which I agreed with and thought they should go talk to Mr. Gomez whose door got shot as well but they brought another attorney who was a specialist in family matters and he took Al aside and said:

"All right, in which ways were you accused of mistreating the child?"

"*The* child—you mean Anthony, you mean *my* child?"

"Whatever. Yes. Not that it matters because this is just a preliminary hearing and I don't think they've got a case but how did you mistreat him?"

I could see it coming in her eyes and I thought it might be bad form—I've always wanted to use that phrase, "bad form," but never had a chance until now—to attack your own attorney so I tugged on Al's arm until she remembered I was there. We went into the courthouse without bothering to answer the attorney.

If I thought it was going to be calmer in the courthouse I was completely wrong. If anything it was worse. I found out something I guess I never knew before which is that people *want* to be on television. Judges and lawyers are just people and they see a camera and they smile and talk a whole lot like everybody else and inside the courthouse there seemed to be more cameras and reporters than there were outside.

"Look over here, Tony, over here. Look this way. When did your mother stop beating you, Tony? Alice, over here, Alice, stand sideways, Alice, give us a profile, Alice . . ."

And on and on and I looked over at Al and I

thought this was horrible and she could see what I was thinking and it made her at first sad and then mad and about then a reporter jostled her and she turned and her eyes did that sparkly thing again and just then I was relieved to see that Ms. Klein had come for what she called "artistic support" and Miles was there too, because Waylon had told him what was happening and he is in the arts and wanted to help and that's when Miles met Al and the electricity thing happened and she forgot about the rude reporters.

I said to Al, "This is Miles, he's my drama teacher who faints sometimes when he reads Shakespeare because it's so good," and she looked at him and smiled and said, "Sometimes

Dickens does the same thing to me," and the spark came and Miles smiled and I smiled and we went into the courtroom and the state had Mrs. Preston there and Mrs. Preston stood up and said to the judge:

"We were called in on a complaint, Your Honor, and during the investigation we were attacked by the defendant and in subsequent investigation it was found that the defendant is a stripper at a place called the Kit Kat Club, where she allowed her son to go and draw pornographic pictures of the other dancers—"

The judge stopped her by holding up a hand and he looked at Al and I thought he was being nice because he smiled although I think really it was probably for the cameras which were all across the back of the courtroom.

"Is all that true?" he asked Al, and her attorney started to rise but Al pushed him back down.

When she stood the room grew quiet except for the clicking of the cameras. She turned to look at all the cameras and then she glanced back at the judge.

"No."

The judge waited for her to continue, and when she didn't, he said, "I beg your pardon?"

"That is a categorically false representation of the facts."

The judge again waited for her to continue, and when she didn't, he sighed. "Let's do this another way. Let's try to find some facts. Are you a stripper?"

Al shook her head. "No. I am a provocative

dancer. But it's more like the story of the Glass Café."

"What story is that?"

Al took a breath and let it out and cameras flicked and flashed. "In Beirut, Lebanon, before it was destroyed by street gangs, when it was the most beautiful city on the Mediterranean, there was a place called the Glass Café. They served coffee in small cups with saucers and men who were professional storytellers would sit and tell stories for listeners who would put coins in the saucers."

"I don't see—"

"The storytellers were very good and they knew just when to hesitate, when to wait in a story to leave the listeners hanging so they could not stand it and would have to put more money in the saucers to hear the rest of the story."

"And the point of all this is . . ."

"I dance the same way. I make people think things, want to know more, and I use the dance to tell the story they want to hear. I am like the Glass Café."

"But you take your clothes off."

"It's part of the dance, part of the story, a costume, a nonuniform that becomes a uniform."

He looked at the ceiling, then back down at the row of cameras, then at Al. "It seems a bit of a stretch."

Al looked back at him, into his eyes. "I

wonder—isn't that robe part of the costume you wear on your job? Isn't that the same thing except that you wear clothes and I take them off to help tell our stories?"

He didn't say anything to this but I saw several people in the audience—the courtroom was packed—nod and smile.

"Let's move on. The complaint says you allowed your son to make pornographic sketches of naked women."

Al shook her head. "That's a judgment call that, frankly, Your Honor, no one here is qualified to make."

His smile vanished. "Oh?"

"No. Number one, most important, they weren't pornographic, not in the least, they were artistically done and I have at least two witnesses who will state so for every one you find who says they were pornographic. Number two, they weren't naked women. They were nude, or one of them was nude, and the rest were wearing varying degrees of clothing."

"Varying degrees . . ." He paused, seemed to consider her words.

"I graduated from college and began graduate school years ago," Al said.

"Then why dance?"

She looked at me and her look softened and then she looked back at the judge. "Because I am privileged to be raising my son alone, with no help from the government or the father, and I can make hundreds of dollars a week dancing. I would love to pursue my doctorate in English literature but it wouldn't pay as well."

He nodded. "Still, there is the question of assault and resisting arrest."

So I had been listening and watching Al do it all and I thought, All right, it's time for me to pull my weight and I stood up from the lawyer's table where I'd been sitting watching and I was going to tell the judge that Al didn't allow people to touch me and that when the cop grabbed me it triggered her Target Response and that was why she hit him with the lamp except that the lawyer next to me, the same one who'd asked Al how she'd abused me but was now watching her with admiring eyes, grabbed on to the back of my shirt and pulled me back down into the chair I guess so I wouldn't interrupt the judge. Which might still have been all right except that just as my butt slammed into the chair, Al turned around and saw that yet another person had their hands on me and her eyes got very glittery again which we were all starting to recognize as a danger sign. Mrs. Preston, who was especially edgy and high-strung, seemed to panic when she saw Al get upset and yelled something else I'd heard the biker say which I think is physically impossible and grabbed her Mace from her purse and ran over to our table and started shooting but got the lawyer instead of Al, who started screaming, the lawyer I mean, about suing somebody or maybe everybody and then the whole courtroom blew up.

CHAPTER SEVEN

Ms. Providge would call this part the "epilogue," which kind of means the part that comes after the main part but I think it's more like a way to tell people how the character arc goes after the story is done and they want to know how everybody turns out.

Al is still Al. Except that she doesn't dance

any longer. The lawyer who got maced turned out to be a little pit bull—or at least that's what Al called him—and he threatened to sue everybody in the court system for himself and for us and in the end it turned out that Mrs. Preston and the cop had exceeded their authority when they came to visit us in the first place, not by visiting us but by assuming that Al was bad without checking first and the system, although I never did find out exactly who that was, offered to settle with us for enough money so that Al could stop dancing and go after her doctorate which is of course going to be on Dickens. Charles Dickens the writer. She says she discovered that he used the idea of dance and the Glass Café concept when he wrote or at least when he lectured and gave performances, to keep people reading his work, and she's going to study that for her thesis and works hard at it except when she goes on a date to see a Shakespeare play with Miles.

I haven't been able to talk Al into letting me have my share of the money yet. She says I'm saving it for college and I say *she's* saving it for my college which isn't the same thing and that might mean that she's Exceeding her Authority as a Parent because she's not taking into account my feelings and what if I go bad and start trying to break the record on stealing bicycles or something and she says she's taking into account the better good for my life and that I'd better watch it or she'll give me so much better good I'll have trouble sitting for a week. So I don't expect that I'll get my hands on it but like Ms. Providge says, we dwell in possibilities and I always have hope.

The same holds true with Melissa. I thought that because we became famous for what Al calls "our fifteen minutes" maybe I would have an easier time of it but she says she's not attracted to me for my fame and left it at that which I think means she *is* attracted to me at least a little so the same as the money: We dwell in possibilities and I always have hope.

Waylon and I still go to the beach and fool around outside and he says he found a way to market some new kind of Rollerblade on the Internet and hopes to be rich by the time he's fifteen or sixteen which I think he just might do.

Carlyle is still with us. He seems to sleep and eat most of the time but comes to be petted and get his ears ruffled and is quiet enough so that the super even saw him and didn't say anything so maybe I have a dog for real. I don't think he's much of a watchdog though because I have a distinct memory of him running for the bathroom when the war broke out in our apartment and not coming out until the smell of Mace was completely gone, which might just mean that he's a really smart dog.

Oh, the biker is still trying to light his

barbecue with strange chemicals. Last week he tried it with paint remover and blew part of a chicken leg completely through the wall and then screamed "Incoming!" and hid under an old couch on his back porch for nearly half a day. At least he didn't have much hair to lose since it hasn't grown back yet from the last time he tried to light the barbecue.

As for me, well, I'm studying art more and Ms. Klein says I'm getting better and I think I am except that I read an article about how math, pure math, might be an art and so I started to look at it that way instead of something just to get through alive and I must admit that it has interest for me because I always thought that math was silly unless you could apply it some way to life and if I can make it an art that will break down the barriers and allow me True Math Freedom.

But I still haven't forgotten about the Corvette.

ABOUT THE AUTHOR

Gary Paulsen is the distinguished author of many critically acclaimed books for young people, including three Newbery Honor books: *The Winter Room, Hatchet* and *Dogsong.* Among his newest Random House books are *How Angel Peterson Got His Name: And Other Outrageous Tales About Extreme Sports; Caught by the Sea: My Life on Boats; Guts: The True Stories Behind* Hatchet *and the Brian Books; The Beet Fields: Memories of a Sixteenth Summer; Brian's Return* and *Brian's Winter* (companions to *Hatchet*) and five books about Francis Tucket's adventures in the Old West. Gary Paulsen has also published fiction and nonfiction for adults, as well as picture books illustrated by his wife, the painter Ruth Wright Paulsen. Their most recent book is *Canoe Days*. The Paulsens live in New Mexico and on the Pacific Ocean.